This Orchard
book belongs to

Kahlman

Thank you for being
in my class this
year and holding
my hand.

Love,
Mrs. Lehrer
2018

For Amy, who walks along the way. M.S.
For Vincent, I am always by your side. B.T.

ORCHARD BOOKS
338 Euston Road, London NW1 3BH
Orchard Books Australia
Level 17/207 Kent Street, Sydney, NSW 2000

First published in 2014 by Orchard Books
First published in paperback 2015 by Orchard Books

ISBN 978 1 40833 317 4

Text © Mark Sperring 2014
Illustrations © Britta Teckentrup 2014

A CIP catalogue record for this book is available from the British Library.

1 3 5 7 9 10 8 6 4 2

Printed in China

Orchard Books is a division of Hachette Children's Books, an Hachette UK company.
www.hachette.co.uk

YOUR HAND
in my hand

MARK SPERRING & BRITTA TECKENTRUP

ORCHARD

Your hand in my hand
is where it belongs,
Your hand in my hand
as we walk along.

The world's full of wonders,
there's so much to see.
I'll find them with you
if you find them with me.

So, why waste a moment?
There's no time to spare!
With your hand in my hand
what wonders we'll share.

We'll splash through the puddles
when rain comes down fast,
And chase after leaves as
the wind whistles past.

We'll gaze up at rainbows . . .
delight in each one!
With your hand in my hand
we'll walk in the sun.

With your hand in my hand,
wherever we go,
Birds will sing sweetly
and flowers will grow.

And all kinds of creatures
will call out 'Hello!'
With your hand in my hand
what friends we will know.

With your hand in my hand
on long hazy days,
We'll paddle and SPLASH
in the warm sunny rays.

And when the days darken
we won't even mind,
With your hand in my hand
what treasures we'll find!

We'll count every
WHOOOOSH!
Every twinkle-bang-POP!
With your hand in my hand
the wonders won't stop!

With your hand in my hand
when winter takes hold,
We'll snuggle up closer
and won't feel the cold.

We'll walk through the seasons,
untouched by the frost . . .

With your hand in my hand . . .

we'll never feel lost.